# JEFF BARTHOLOMEUSZ

# The Perfect Fit

## AUSTIN MACAULEY PUBLISHERS™
LONDON • CAMBRIDGE • NEW YORK • SHARJAH

A CIP catalogue record for this title is available from the British Library.

ISBN 9781035831807 (Paperback)
ISBN 9781035831814 (Hardback)
ISBN 9781035831821 (ePub-e-book)

www.austinmacauley.com

First Published 2023
Austin Macauley Publishers Ltd®
1 Canada Square
Canary Wharf
London
E14 5AA

This book is dedicated to Nic,
Jack & Tom, for their
inspirational love and support.

Hermie the hermit crab was tired
of his shell.
It was crooked and beyond repair,
as far he could tell.

To find something special, far and wide
he'd have to roam.
A shelter, a refuge, a place to call his home.

Suddenly on the horizon, right before his eyes, he came upon a brand new home completely by surprise.

"Oh magnificent palace," he thought, this had to be it!

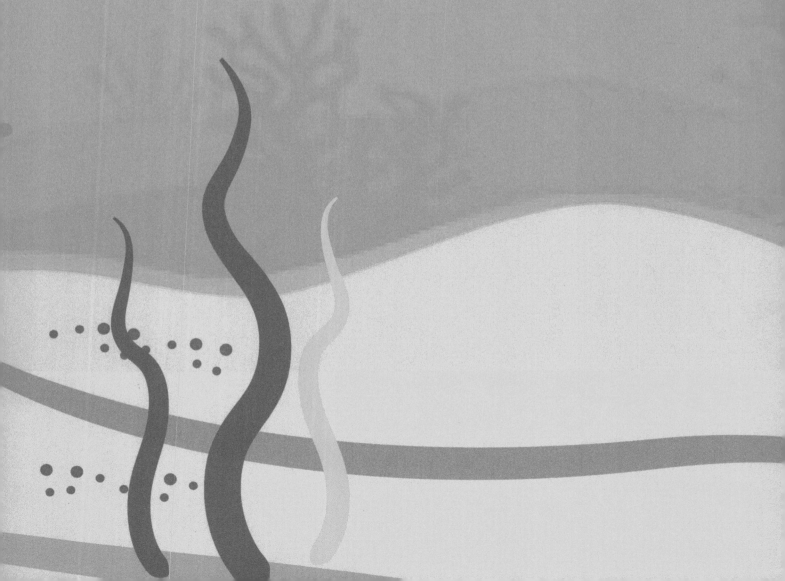

But the bottle wasn't exactly going to be the perfect fit.

And so his search continued to find a new abode.
One that was appropriate, one he could call home.

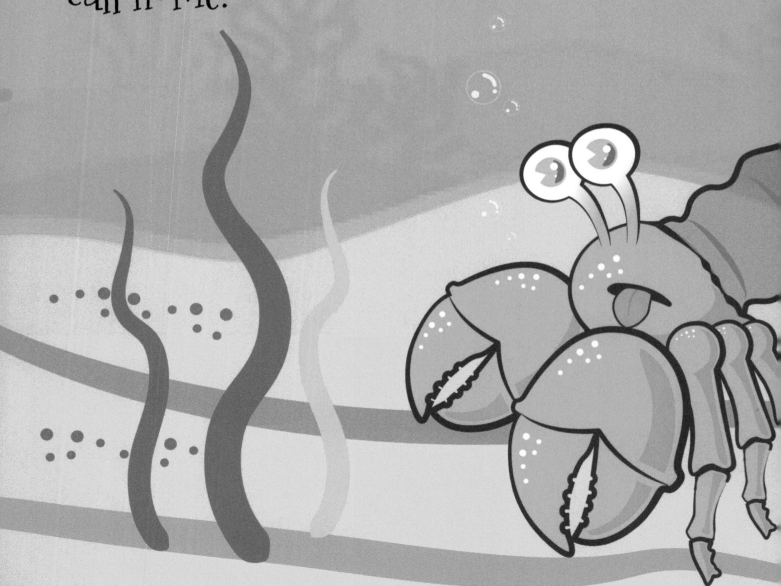

Then floating in the distance, like a transparent, waving flag, wobbling and silent was a plastic Ziplock bag.

This seemed to have potential, with versatility and size.

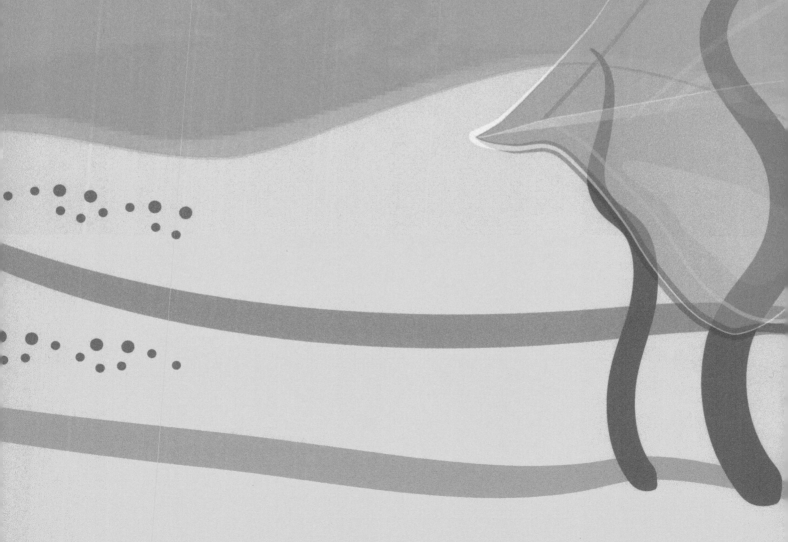

A dream home with
room to move,
an architectural
prize!

But once he'd tried it on he groaned and his brows began to knit.

The bag was too transparent and not the perfect fit!

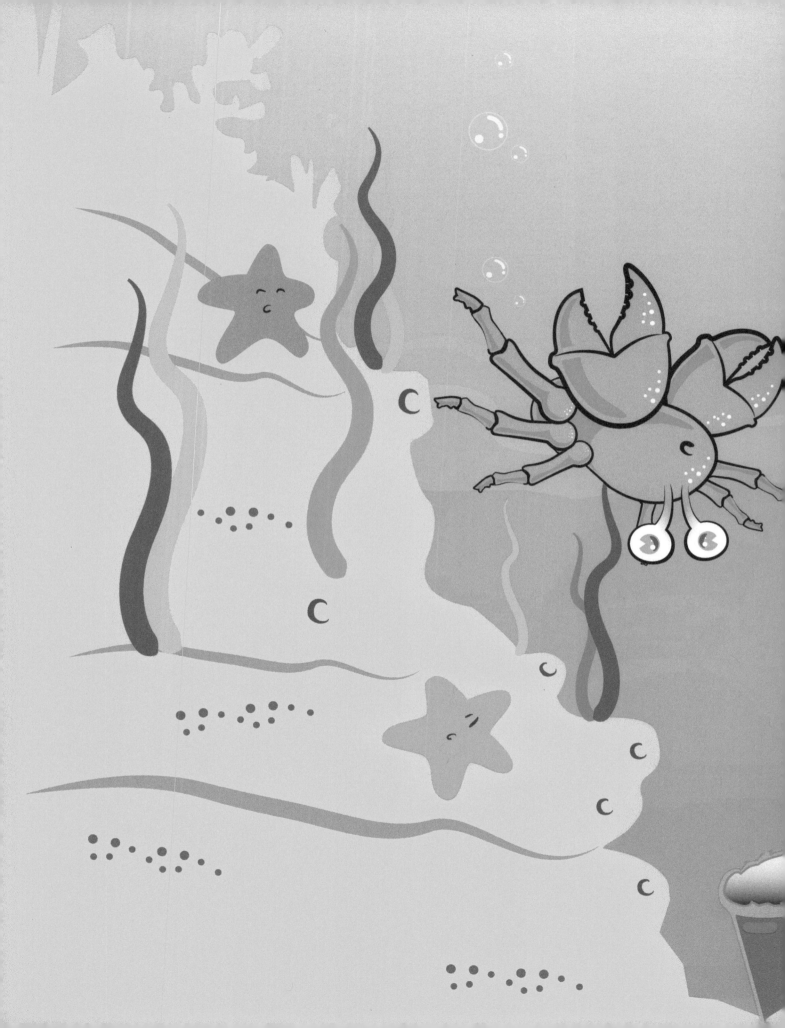

He climbed atop some coral, but tumbled to the sand,

And when he'd found his footing, it was inside a can!

But the edges of the can were sharp and painful to the touch.

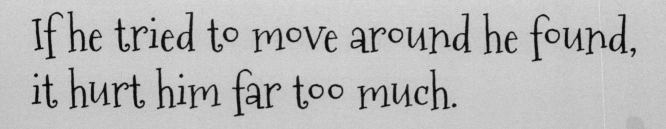

If he tried to move around he found,
it hurt him far too much.

So he kicked the can idea and
continued on his quest,
to find the perfect domicile,
the one that would be best!

And then there was a castle, so perfect for a prince!

But it turned out to be a hassle and he wasn't quite convinced.

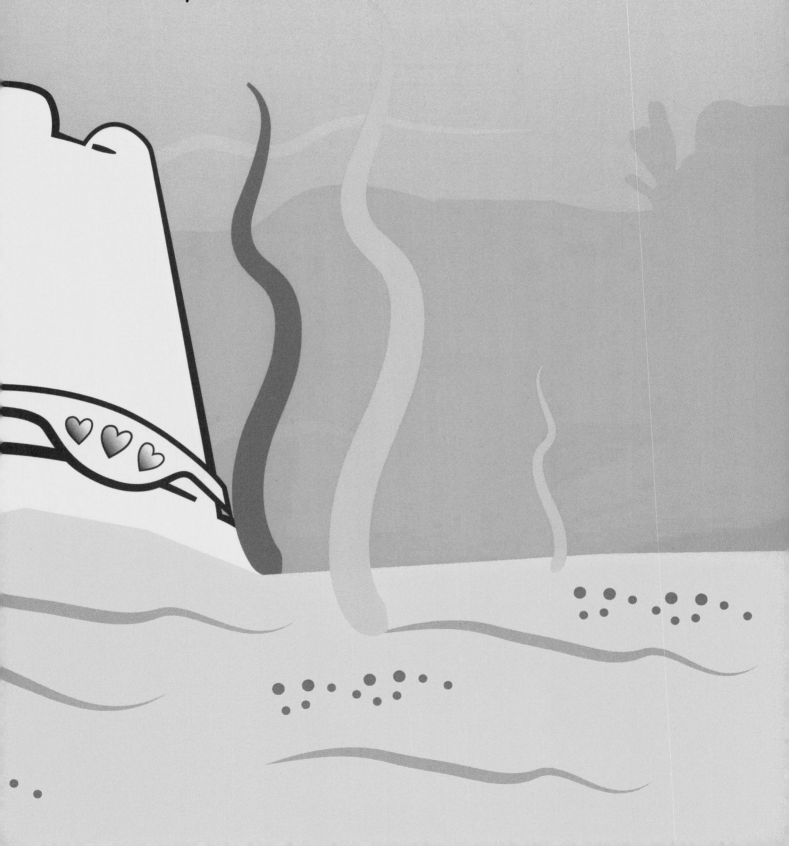

And try as he might he couldn't make it work.

So in frustration he said, "Bucket, I'm outta here!" and continued on his search.

Then suddenly it hit him, so obvious
to see.

All these 'houses' were just rubbish and
should not be in the sea.

What he needed wasn't man-made or manufactured, not one bit.

But what Nature had intended to be his perfect fit!

## About the Author

Jeff is a first-time author who made up this
story to read to his children on a beach
holiday when his boys found some shells
which should have been empty but weren't.
Turns out they were hermit crabs and wanted
to get back to their home in the ocean.

Ingram Content Group UK Ltd.
Milton Keynes UK
UKHW050049140723
425088UK00003B/48

9 781035 831814